Darcey the Dance Diva Fairy

by Daisy Meadows

Join the **Rainbow Magic Reading Challenge!**

Read the story and collect your fairy points to climb the Reading Rainbow at the back of the book.

This book is worth 5 points.

The Fairyland Palace
Cooke Football Stadium
Rachel's House
Tippington Town
TIPPINGTON FESTIVAL
CUPCAKES
Sweets
POP CORN
Hook a Duck
Tippington Funfair

Jack Frost's Ice Castle
Swan Theatre
THE SWAN THEATRE
Funky Feet Dance Studios
Tippington Ice Rink

Who likes talent shows? Not me!
So, goblins, listen carefully,
Each Showtime Fairy has a star,
Their magic glitters near and far.

Now do exactly as I say,
And steal these magical stars away,
Then, when our wicked work is done,
We can spoil all showtime fun!

Contents

Funky Feet!

"*The Funky Feet Dance Studios,*" Kirsty read out as she stared up at the pink and blue neon sign on top of the modern glass and steel building. She grinned. "That's a *brilliant* name for a dance studio, isn't it, Rachel?"

Rachel laughed. "Yes, it makes you feel like dancing, doesn't it? Look, Kirsty, the Tippington School team is already here."

And she pointed at the school minibus in the car park.

"We should be just in time to see them rehearse before they take part in the dance auditions."

Every day during the half-term holiday, local schools, including Rachel's, were taking part in auditions in magic, drama, acrobatics, dance, singing and ice skating.

The Tippington Variety Show was being held at the end of half-term week, and the organisers were choosing the best acts to perform in the show. The money raised would be used to pay for an adventure playground, a bandstand and an outdoor theatre in the town's Oval Park. Today it was the dance auditions, and the girls had come along to support Tippington School. Several of Rachel's friends were taking part in the auditions.

"I'm going to cheer as loudly as I can when Tippington School perform their street dance routine!" Kirsty said as they went through the automatic glass doors into the building.

"I'm having a really great time staying with you this half-term, Rachel. It's *so* exciting with all these auditions going on."

"And that's not the only thing that's going on!" Rachel whispered, flashing Kirsty a secret smile. "It's even *more* exciting because we're having another amazing fairy adventure!"

On the very first day of the auditions, Madison the Magic Show Fairy had appeared very unexpectedly and asked Rachel and Kirsty for help. The girls had agreed immediately, and Madison had taken them straight to Fairyland to meet the other six Showtime Fairies.

The Showtime Fairies' task was to

make sure that everyone in both the human and the fairy worlds could use their showtime talents to the full, and they did this with the help of the magical stars fixed to the tips of their wands.

But while the Showtime Fairies had been rehearsing for their own Variety Show, mean Jack Frost had ruined everything. He'd ordered his goblins to steal the Showtime Fairies' magical stars and hide them away in the human world. Now the stars were missing, it meant that both humans and fairies had lost their showtime skills. So far, Rachel and Kirsty had helped the Showtime Fairies find three of their stars, and they'd managed to save the magic show, drama and acrobatics auditions from being completely ruined.

But there were still four stars left to find before the Variety Show at the end of the week. Rachel and Kirsty knew that if they didn't find *all* the stars by then, the show would be a disaster.

"I wonder if the goblins will be here today?" Kirsty said to Rachel in a low voice. To make things worse, Jack Frost's goblins had been turning up to the auditions, pretending they were from a school called Icy Towers. Their aim was to use the magic of the Showtime Fairies' stars to cheat and win the auditions, but so far Rachel, Kirsty and the fairies had foiled their plans.

"I'm sure they'll be here," Rachel replied, "along with Darcey the Dance Diva Fairy's magic star!" She glanced across the lobby. "Look, there's Miss Patel and the Tippington School team."

Miss Patel, the teacher organising the auditions, was at the reception desk, registering the team with the person in charge. A large, squashy bag lay at her feet, and Rachel guessed it was packed with the team's costumes for the auditions.

The dancers who were taking part stood chatting nearby. They were all wearing T-shirts, joggers and trainers, ready for their rehearsal.

"There are my friends, Jaydon and Annie," Rachel told Kirsty. "Come and say hello."

"Hey, Rachel," Jaydon called, his face breaking into a smile as he spotted the girls. "Thanks for coming to support us."

"I wouldn't miss it for anything!" Rachel exclaimed. "Kirsty, meet Jaydon and Annie."

"We've heard lots about you, Kirsty," Annie said with a twinkle in her eyes. "Rachel's always talking about you!"

Kirsty grinned. "Good luck with the audition," she said. "Rachel and I will be cheering for you all the way!"

"Listen, please, everyone." Miss Patel came over to them. "The dance theatre where the auditions will take place is on the ground floor, and the dressing-rooms and practice studios are upstairs."

Just then she noticed Rachel and Kirsty. "Thanks for coming along to support us, girls," Miss Patel told them with a smile. "We can always use an extra pair of hands! Right, follow me."

Miss Patel led the team up a sweeping chrome staircase. Rachel and Kirsty joined Jaydon and Annie at the back of the line.

"How have the rehearsals been going so far?" Rachel asked.

Jaydon and Annie both looked a bit depressed.

"Not so good," Jaydon replied with a sigh. "We've been practising *really* hard all week, but somehow we still can't get things right."

"It's almost like we have two left feet!" Annie added, biting her lip.

Rachel and Kirsty didn't say anything, but they glanced at each other knowingly. This was because Darcey the Dance Diva Fairy's star was missing.

"Ah, here we are." Miss Patel stopped outside a dressing-room with a sign pinned to the door reading *Tippington School.* "Let's go in and lay the costumes out, ready for the auditions, and then we'll go and rehearse. We're in the Hip-Hop Hideaway studio on the third floor."

"Kirsty and I could lay out the costumes, Miss Patel," Rachel suggested as the teacher opened the dressing-room door. "It would save you some time."

"What a good idea!" Miss Patel said gratefully. "Thank you, girls. The costumes are labelled with everyone's names." She put the bag down on the dressing-room floor and turned to the dancers. "Let's go, everyone. We still need to do some *serious* rehearsing to get everything right before the audition."

"Good luck," Kirsty said to Annie as the dancers followed Miss Patel out.

"Thanks," Annie replied, "We'll do our best." But Kirsty could see that she didn't look very hopeful.

"We've got to find Darcey's star before the dance audition!" Rachel said urgently when Miss Patel and the dancers had gone.

"Yes, but we have to wait for the magic to come to *us*," Kirsty reminded her. "Now that we're on our own, maybe we'll meet Darcey. She'll be here somewhere, looking for her star."

Rachel unzipped the big bag and she and Kirsty began taking out the costumes. The team would be wearing baggy black and silver trousers, black T-shirts with *Tippington School* on the front in sparkly silver letters, glittering silver baseball caps and matching trainers. Carefully, the girls began to lay out the clothes in neat piles around the dressing-room.

"They're going to look great, aren't they?" Rachel said, admiring the sparkly silver trainers as she placed them with the rest of Annie's outfit.

Kirsty didn't reply. Frowning, she had her head to one side as if she was listening hard for something.

"What's the matter?" Rachel asked.

"I thought I heard a strange rattling noise," Kirsty murmured. "Listen! There it is again!"

This time Rachel heard it, too. "I think it's coming from the dressing-table," she said.

The only thing on the dressing-table was a large box labelled *Stage Make-up*. The girls went over to it and Kirsty opened the lid. A faint cloud of pink blusher and blue eye shadow wafted out and in the middle of it fluttered a tiny fairy.

"It's Darcey the Dance Diva Fairy!" Rachel cried, delighted.

Strictly Goblin Dancing!

"Hello, girls!" Darcey looked thrilled to see them. Shaking a mist of pink dust from her blonde hair, she flew down to hover in front of the girls. She wore an aqua-coloured dress with swaying fringes and was wearing gold high-heeled dance shoes and a pretty hairband with a feather on it. "I've been looking for you!"

"And *we* were hoping to see *you*!" Rachel told her. "The Tippington dance team aren't very happy at the moment. Everything's going wrong."

Darcey's wings drooped sadly. "Yes, and it will be the same for *all* the teams," she said with a sigh, "unless we find my star before the auditions take place!"

"What does your star look like, Darcey?" asked Kirsty.

"Oh, it's absolutely beautiful!" Darcey said with a big smile. "It shimmers with rainbow colours and it has a picture of a ballet shoe on it."

"We haven't seen any goblins around the dressing-rooms, so maybe we should go to the rehearsal studios and check those out," Rachel suggested.

"Great idea," Darcey agreed. She fluttered down to hide inside one of Kirsty's pockets, and the girls left the dressing-room.

The practice studios were on the floors above the dressing-rooms, so Rachel and Kirsty climbed up another staircase. They found themselves in a corridor lined with studios, each with a different name.

"*Jive Junction*." Kirsty read out. The door of the *Jive Junction* studio was ajar and the girls could hear music. Hoping no-one spotted them, they peeped inside the studio, looking for Darcey's star.

Rachel and Kirsty saw a large, light, spacious room with mirrors on all four walls and a barre along one side. There was a team from one of the other schools in there, practising a rock 'n' roll routine.

As the girls watched, one of the boys attempted to spin his partner round, but he spun her too hard and the girl flew across the room. With a shriek of surprise, she clattered into one of the other couples and almost knocked them both over.

The next studio was called *Pirouette Place*. Rachel and Kirsty looked in and saw a team of ballroom dancers practising the waltz and the foxtrot.

But the girls could see that they were treading on each others' toes, and when the couples twirled around, they couldn't seem to stop until they got dizzy. And then they stumbled and almost fell.

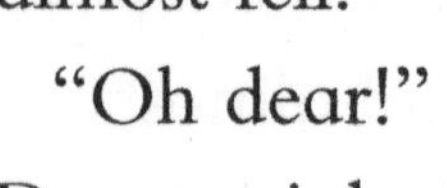

"Oh dear!" Darcey sighed, looking very upset. "There's no sign of my star here either. And everyone's getting into *such* a muddle!"

Rachel looked at the sign on the door of the next studio. "*The Hip-Hop Hideaway*," she read out. "That's where Tippington School are rehearsing. They must have started by now because I can hear music."

Darcey ducked out of sight again as the girls went inside the studio. But neither Rachel nor Kirsty could believe what they saw!

The Tippington team hadn't started rehearsing yet. They were standing with Miss Patel at the side of the room, watching another team of four dancing around the studio floor.

Unlike the other teams, Rachel could see that this group of dancers were wonderful, and they weren't putting a foot wrong. The four boys were wearing heavy stage make-up, and they were all dressed in brightly coloured costumes decorated with sequins, ribbons and feathers. They were showing off a strange mix of dance styles. There was a ballerina in a white tutu and a large head-dress of white feathers pirouetting around the floor. A salsa dancer in a red ruffled shirt, sparkly waistcoat and broad-brimmed black hat was wiggling his hips as he stared at himself in the mirrors, and a tap dancer in a top hat and tails clicked his way across the studio. Meanwhile, a street-dancer in a black T-shirt, baggy trousers, trainers and a baseball cap was doing a fantastic backspin on the floor.

"Look at the street-dancer's T-shirt!" Kirsty whispered in dismay. "It says the name of the team on the front – Icy Towers! It's the goblins!"

"And they're dancing so well, they *must* have Darcey's star!" Rachel added.

Kirsty in a Spin

Just then there was a break in the music and Miss Patel stepped forward.

"Sorry to interrupt," she said with a frown, "But this studio has been allocated to Tippington School. You'll have to go downstairs and register, then you'll be given your own studio to rehearse in."

The goblins started muttering crossly to each other.

"Rachel and Kirsty, could you show the Icy Towers boys downstairs to the registration desk?" Miss Patel went on.

The girls glanced at each other. This could be the perfect opportunity to get Darcey's star away from the goblins!

"Of course we will, Miss Patel," Rachel agreed.

"Don't want to go and register," the ballet dancer goblin said sulkily.

"We were here first!" snapped the salsa goblin, glaring at Rachel and Kirsty.

"Oh, but if you don't register, you won't be able to take part in the auditions," Kirsty said.

"And that would be a real shame, because you're such brilliant dancers!" added Rachel. She and Kirsty went over to the door, hoping the goblins would follow.

The goblins grinned proudly.

"Yes, we are, aren't we?" agreed the tap-dancer goblin. And he tapped his way out of the studio after the girls. The other goblins followed him, the ballerina on her toes and the salsa goblin shimmying his hips.

Finally the street-dancer goblin back-flipped through the door. As Rachel and Kirsty led the way down the corridor, the goblins danced along behind them.

"Let's dance!" the salsa goblin shouted.

To Kirsty's surprise, he grabbed her hand and began to twirl her around in a fast salsa spin.

"Stop it!" Kirsty gasped breathlessly as she began to feel dizzy, but the goblin wouldn't let go. He spun Kirsty around even faster. And suddenly, with a tiny cry of surprise, Darcey was flung out of Kirsty's pocket and went flying through the air.

"A fairy!" yelled the ballerina goblin furiously. "Look! A pesky fairy!"

"They're trying to trick us into giving the magic star back!" the street-dancer goblin hollered.

"Catch us if you can!" declared the tap-dancer goblin, poking his tongue out at Rachel, Kirsty and Darcey. And with that, the four goblins ran down a corridor and through another door.

"After them!" Rachel shouted.

But when the three friends rushed through the door themselves, all they could see was another staircase.

"Which way did the goblins go?" Kirsty panted. "Up or down?"

"There are four other floors in the building," Rachel said, dismayed. "They could be *anywhere*."

"How will we possibly manage to search all these rooms and find the goblins before the auditions?" Kirsty sighed.

"Don't despair, girls." Darcey raised her wand. "We need some help. And I know exactly where to find it!"

Then Darcey waved her wand and with a shower of fairy dust, she turned the girls into fairies and whisked them off to Fairyland!

Search for a Star

When the cloud of fairy dust had vanished, Rachel and Kirsty found themselves at the outdoor theatre in the Fairyland Palace gardens.

"Look, girls," said Darcey, pointing her wand at the stage. "The Dance Fairies are rehearsing for our Variety Show in honour of King Oberon and Queen Titania."

Rachel and Kirsty could see their old friends Bethany the Ballet Fairy, Jade the Disco Fairy, Rebecca the Rock 'n' Roll Fairy, Tasha the Tap Dance Fairy, Jessica the Jazz Fairy, Saskia the Salsa Fairy and Imogen the Ice Dance Fairy on the stage. As the girls and Darcey watched Bethany pirouetting around the stage, they saw her ballet shoe ribbons come loose. Bethany and Jade tripped over the ribbons, falling in different directions!

"Sorry, Jade!" Bethany gasped.

"Don't worry, Bethany," Jade replied glumly, "I can't get my steps right anyway!"

At that moment Imogen the Ice Dance Fairy, who was twirling around on her little ice rink, slipped and fell over.

"Imogen, are you all right?" Darcey called, flying over to her. Rachel and Kirsty followed.

"I'm fine." Imogen climbed to her feet. "But that's the fifth time I've fallen over this morning!"

"This is just what's happening back at *The Funky Feet Dance Studios*," Rachel murmured to Kirsty.

"We've all prepared some wonderful dance routines for the show," Rebecca the Rock 'n' Roll Fairy told Rachel and Kirsty sadly, "But nothing's going right for *any* of us!"

"That's why we're here," Darcey replied. "We're on the trail of my star! But the goblins are hiding out in the dance studios and we need to find them quickly. Will you help?"

"Of course we will!" the Dance Fairies chorused.

"Let's go right away," Saskia the Salsa Fairy added.

All eight fairies waved their wands. Immediately, a sparkling mist of magical fairy dust sent them spinning off to the human world, taking Rachel and Kirsty with them.

When they arrived, Rachel and Kirsty were still fairy-sized. The girls and the other fairies were all hidden among the frilly folds of a pink tutu hanging on a rack of costumes.

"We're back in the Tippington School dressing-room," Darcey said, peeping out between the rustling folds of material.

"Girls, we'll stay together and search this floor while the Dance Fairies look downstairs."

The Dance Fairies immediately zoomed out of the dressing-room door.

Meanwhile, Darcey and the girls flew up and down the corridors, checking out the other dressing-rooms. But the goblins were nowhere to be seen.

"Let's go up to the next floor and have a look around the dance studios," Kirsty suggested. "The goblins may have gone back there after we left."

The three friends flew up the staircase to the *Jive Junction, Pirouette Place and Hip-Hop Hideaway* studios. The team in the *Jive Junction* studio were just leaving, so Darcey and the girls hid behind a curtain in the corridor until they'd gone. Then they flew into the studio, looking for the star.

"Look at our reflections," Kirsty remarked as they whizzed around the four mirrored walls. "It looks like there are *twelve* fairies flying around!"

"The star isn't here," said Darcey, disappointed. "But it sounds like the other rehearsals are finishing, too, so we'll be able to search the other studios."

"If the rehearsals have finished, that means there isn't much time before the auditions start," Rachel pointed out anxiously.

Darcey nodded, also looking worried. "My star's definitely close by," she said, "I can *feel* it!"

Quickly, Darcey and the girls searched the other studios on that floor, but found nothing.

"I'll call the Dance Fairies back and then we'll search the other floors," Darcey said. Then, writing with her wand in the air, she spelt out the word *Return* in sparkling fairy dust. Just a few seconds later, all the Dance Fairies reappeared.

None of them had found the star.

"We must hurry," Darcey told everyone as they flew up the stairs to the next floor. "This is a race against time!"

As they reached the top of the stairs, Rachel and Kirsty heard the sound of loud disco music.

"*The Disco Den*," Rachel read out as all ten fairies hovered outside the studio door. Meanwhile Kirsty peeped in through the open door.

"The goblins are here!" Kirsty whispered.

Darcey, Rachel and the Dance Fairies joined Kirsty to peer inside. *The Disco Den* had four mirrored walls and a barre, like the other studios, but there was also an enormous glitter ball hanging from the ceiling.

The goblins were standing in front of one mirrored wall, practising their dance moves. They were so caught up in admiring themselves that they didn't notice the ten fairies fly silently into the room. Darcey pointed at the glitter ball, and she, Rachel, Kirsty and the Dance Fairies perched on top of it.

"Ballet's the best!" said the ballerina goblin, standing on his points. He danced across the room, leaping and turning gracefully as he did so.

"Salsa's super!" said the salsa goblin firmly, "It's much better than ballet." And he began snapping his fingers and shaking his hips.

"I bet none of you can do *this*!" the street-dancer boasted. He took off his baseball cap and laid it carefully on the ground. Then he stood on his head and performed a brilliant head spin.

Suddenly a shimmer of light from inside the baseball cap caught Kirsty's eye. She looked a little more closely and saw a star glittering in the light, and her heart began to thump with excitement.

"I can see the magic star!" Kirsty whispered to Darcey, Rachel and the others. "It's inside the street-dancer's baseball cap!"

Fairies, Fairies Everywhere!

Darcey, Rachel and the Dance Fairies stared down at the cap.

"Well spotted, Kirsty!" Darcey murmured, her eyes shining. "Now all we have to do is fly down and get it back!"

"You three are losers compared to me!" the tap-dancer goblin boasted.

He held out his black and white cane, twirling it around. "I get a cane to dance with – and that makes me special!" He tap-danced across the floor just as the fairies prepared to grab the star.

Suddenly, the tap-dancer goblin struck a pose and then tossed his cane high up into the air as part of his routine. It hit the glitter ball and set it swaying wildly, tipping the ten fairies right off. With startled gasps, Rachel, Kirsty, Darcey and the Dance Fairies tumbled downwards. The goblins saw them and yelled with fright.

"Fairies!" shouted the salsa goblin as the tap-dancer goblin caught his cane as it fell down again. "Hundreds of them!"

For a moment Kirsty didn't understand what the goblin meant. But then she realised that she and the other fairies were reflected not just in the mirrored walls, but also in the glitter ball. It *did* look like there were lots of them flying around the studio!

"Quick!" shrieked the ballerina goblin, "Get the star before they do!"

The street-dancer goblin dashed over, grabbed his baseball cap and stuck it firmly on top of his head with the star still inside. Then, holding the cap on with both hands, he ran over to join the other goblins who were huddled together in one corner.

"Get away!" yelled the salsa goblin, hitting out at the reflections swirling around them.

"Let's make a run for it," the ballerina goblin suggested.

"No, there are too many fairies," the tap-dancer goblin shrieked, "We'll never make it to the door!"

"Keep flying around the studio, everyone," Darcey whispered. "That way the goblins will believe there are too many of us for them to escape!"

"But how are we going to get the star back?" asked Jessica the Jazz Fairy as they all continued to circle the studio.

"Oh!" Rachel said suddenly, "I have an idea that might just work!" Quickly she whispered her plan to the others, and they all nodded in agreement.

Rachel and Kirsty fluttered down to the floor, and then Darcey scattered a shower of sparkling fairy dust over them. Instantly, the girls shot up to their normal size. The goblins gasped with fear and glared at them.

"Look, we just wanted to tell you that we think you're *brilliant* dancers!" Rachel said with a big smile. "And the Dance Fairies have come here specially to teach you a fantastic new routine to impress the judges at the auditions." She beckoned to Darcey and the other fairies, and they flew down to join them.

All four goblins looked very suspicious.

"Why would the silly fairies want to help *us*?" snorted the ballerina goblin.

"Because they think you can win the audition – *if* you do what they say," Kirsty replied. "At the moment you're all doing different dances. You'll have to perform the *same* routine if you want to win."

"And Kirsty and I will be your backing dancers," Rachel added. "All the top stars have them!"

The goblins looked at each other.

"Well, all right then," the tap-dancer goblin said with a scowl. "But don't try any tricks!"

The goblins lined up in front of one of the mirrors, and Darcey and the Dance Fairies perched on the barre. Meanwhile, Rachel and Kirsty hurried to stand in front of the goblins.

"Just follow our instructions," Darcey called. "Start with a right kick!"

"And then a left," Jessica the Jazz Fairy chimed in.

"Shake your hips and step forward and back," said Jade the Disco Fairy.

"And don't forget to point your toes," Bethany the Ballet Fairy reminded them.

"You're doing brilliantly!" Rachel called as she and Kirsty copied the goblins' moves.

"You're total stars!" Tasha the Tap Dance Fairy told the goblins, and they preened themselves even more as they danced. "Come on, clap your hands above your heads!"

"High kicks!" shouted Rebecca the Rock 'n' Roll Fairy. The goblins did as they were told.

"Head spins!" instructed Darcey. Rachel and Kirsty glanced at each other. That was their cue!

"Oh, good," said the street-dancer goblin gleefully, "I'm going to be the best at this!" And he took off his baseball cap. Rachel and Kirsty could see the star shimmering inside.

"Grab it, Kirsty!" Rachel whispered.

The girls rushed forward, one on each side of the goblin, and tried to snatch the cap out of his hands.

"Stop that!" the goblin roared, trying to fight Rachel and Kirsty off. But as he did so, the star fell out of the baseball cap and onto the floor. Immediately all the goblins and all the fairies swooped down to capture the star. But the mirrors and the glitter ball were reflecting the shimmering star hundreds of times over, and it was difficult to tell which was the real star and which was a sparkling reflection.

"Where's the *real* star?" Darcey gasped, hunting around on the floor. "It's gone!"

But luckily both Rachel and Kirsty had fixed their eyes on the star as it fell from the baseball cap. They knew *exactly* where it was!

Rachel rushed forward and picked the star up from the floor. Then she ran to the door with Kirsty close behind her.

"Over here, Darcey!" Rachel called from the doorway, holding the star aloft.

Darcey's face lit up as she saw her star in Rachel's hand. She zoomed over to the girls, followed by the Dance Fairies, and they all rushed out of the studio.

"Where's the star gone?" the salsa goblin wailed as Rachel, Kirsty, Darcey and the other fairies hurried off along the corridor. "There were *hundreds* of stars here a moment ago!"

The girls and the fairies went quickly down the stairs that led down to the Tippington School dressing-room.

The dressing-room door stood open and straightaway Rachel saw that the Tippington School

costumes had gone.

"The team must have changed and gone downstairs, ready to perform," Kirsty exclaimed, closing the door firmly so that the goblins couldn't come after them. "The auditions must be about to start!"

"Attention, everyone!" At that very moment the announcer spoke over the loudspeaker in the dressing-room, making the girls and the fairies jump.

"The auditions are about to start in the dance theatre on the ground floor. Please take your seats."

Beaming, Rachel handed the sparkling star to Darcey. As soon as Darcey touched it, it shrank down to fairy-size and she fitted it on to her wand. The girls and the Dance Fairies clapped and cheered.

"We did it, girls!" Darcey beamed, hugging her wand with delight. "Well done, everyone."

Suddenly the sound of music filled the dressing-room.

"Oh, this is *Street Dance Magic*," said Rachel, snapping her fingers to the beat. "Tippington School are dancing to this track."

"Let's have our own dance party right here in the dressing-room!" suggested Darcey, and she back-flipped through the air, one after another. The girls watched in delight as the other seven fairies joined in, doing an amazing routine of head spins, backspins, body glides and somersaults. As they whizzed through the air, they left trails of sparkling fairy dust behind them. Rachel and Kirsty joined in, too, dancing around the empty dressing-room until the music stopped.

"Listen to that applause!" Kirsty gasped as they heard the audience clapping in the theatre downstairs. "Tippington School must have done really well."

"Everyone can enjoy dancing again now that Darcey's got her star back!" Rachel added with a smile.

Now it's time for Kirsty and Rachel to help...

Amelia the Singing Fairy

Read on for a sneak peek...

WELCOME TO TIPPINGTON FESTIVAL! read a large banner strung above the entrance to a plaza at the edge of Tippington village. Kirsty Tate and her best friend Rachel Walker went into the festival site, with Rachel's parents close behind. Kirsty was staying with Rachel's family for a week over half-term, and the two girls were having a very exciting time so far. But then again, exciting things *always* seemed to happen when Kirsty and Rachel got together!

"This looks great," Kirsty said, gazing around. There were all sorts of food and craft stalls along the sides of the plaza, as well as dancers, singers and jugglers performing in different areas.

"Look at the fountains!" Rachel said, pointing to where three jets of water shot up inside an ornate white stone base in the centre of the square. Colourful lights played across the falling water so that the fountains appeared to be shimmering every colour of the rainbow.

"They look almost magical, don't they?" Rachel's dad said, and the two girls gave each other a secret smile...

Read Amelia the Singing Fairy
to find out what adventures are in store for
Kirsty and Rachel!

Meet the Showtime Fairies

Collect them all to find out how Kirsty and Rachel help their magical friends to save the Tippington Variety Show!

www.rainbowmagicbooks.co.uk

Meet the fairies, play games
and get sneak peeks at
the latest books!

www.rainbowmagicbooks.co.uk

There's fairy fun for everyone on
our wonderful website.
You'll find great activities, competitions, stories and
fairy profiles, and also a special newsletter.

Get 30% off all Rainbow Magic books at

www.rainbowmagicbooks.co.uk

Enter the code RAINBOW at the checkout.
Offer ends 31 December 2013.

Offer valid in United Kingdom and Republic of Ireland only.

Competition!

The Baby Animal Rescue Fairies have created
a special competition just for you!
In the back of each book in the series there will be
a question for you to answer.
Once you have collected all the books and all
seven answers, go online and enter the competition!

We will put all the correct entries into a draw and select
a winner to receive a special Rainbow Magic Goody Bag,
featuring lots of treats for you and your fairy friends.
The winner will also star in a new Rainbow Magic story!

What is the name of the Snow Fairy in the Weather Fairies series?

_ _ _ _ _ _ _

Enter online now at www.rainbowmagicbooks.co.uk

No purchase required. Only one entry per child.
Two prize draws will take place on 1st April 2014 and 2nd July 2014. Alternatively readers can send the answer on a postcard to: Rainbow Magic, Baby Animal Rescue Fairies Competition, Orchard Books, 338 Euston Road, London, NW1 3BH. Australian readers can write to: Rainbow Magic, Baby Animal Rescue Fairies Competition, Hachette Children's Books, level 17/207 Kent St, Sydney, NSW 2000. E-mail: childrens.books@hachette.com.au.
New Zealand readers should write to:
Rainbow Magic, Baby Animal Rescue Fairies Competition,
4 Whetu Place, Mairangi Bay, Auckland, NZ

Meet the Sporty Fairies

Join Rachel and Kirsty as they help the Sporty Fairies to foil Jack Frost's naughty plot to mess up the Fairyland Olympics!

www.rainbowmagicbooks.co.uk

Meet the Music Fairies

Jack Frost has stolen the Music Fairies' magical notes! Kirsty and Rachel must get them back or music will never sound sweet again.

www.rainbowmagicbooks.co.uk